MW00877207

THE BLUE DEMON

PRAISE FOR THE BLUE DEMON

Somewhat casually we started reading The Blue Demon and practically before we knew it we had FINISHED THE ENTIRE BOOK! It's been decades since we immersed ourselves in (literally) the horror fiction of William Hope Hodgson, Edgar Allan Poe and H.P. Lovecraft, but this short novel (with a definite original twist) ranks with the best writings of those ground-breaking explorers of the dark depths of psychological nightmarishness just on the borderlands adjacent to utter madness. We highly recommend this book!

– V.Vale, RE/Search, Search&Destroy Founder,
San Francisco CA

The Blue Demon is a very viscous adventure story. The brooding beginning, sensual language, and strapping valiant heroes are pure Gothic Victorian– but the seething ocean water and surreal preoccupations of the talented enemy remind me of Max Ernst. This tale is exquisitely fun and weird. It will suck you in with the salty strength of a mighty monster wrapping its tentacle around your brain!

– Colleen McKee, author of *Nine Kinds of Wrong*,
Oakland CA

The mysterious writer Youssef Alaoui-Fdili has a good grip of traditional sea tales. Given his original verve and mastery, indicative of both fan and connoisseur, he has the remarkable gift to renew the genre and insert it into the heart of modern readership. So welcome aboard! The Blue Demon is a cult hit!

– Tsunami bOOKS, Paris

I read The Blue Demon last night. A fantastic read! A wonderfully textured tale with mystic undertones and visceral horror. I'm truly a fan! And, being an agoraphobic myself, I can relate to the terror rising from the murky depths. I'll be looking forward to reading more from this author.

– Mark C. Morris, *Blue Ruins* Horror Blogger

The Blue Demon

Youssef Alaoui Fdili

THE BLUE DEMON

YOUSSEF ALAOUI FDILI

"Maelstrom" cover illustration by Alberto Martini 1902-1909
for *Tales of Edgar Allan Poe*

Paper Press Books & Assoc. Publishing Co.

ISBN-13: 978-1475103915
ISBN-10: 1475103913

A PAPER PRESS BOOK.

Thanks Ma!

A DESCENT INTO THE MAELSTRÖM

This 'little cliff' arose, a sheer unobstructed precipice of black shining rock, some fifteen or sixteen hundred feet from the world of crags beneath us.

Nothing would have tempted me to be within half a dozen yards of its brink. In truth so deeply was I excited by the perilous position of my companion, that I fell at full length upon the ground, clung to the shrubs around me, and dared not even glance upward at the sky – while I struggled in vain to divest myself of the idea that the very foundations of the mountain were in danger from the fury of the winds. It was long before I could reason myself into sufficient courage to sit up and look out into the distance.

"You must get over these fancies," said the guide, "for I have brought you here that you might have the best possible view of the scene of that event I mentioned – and to tell you the whole story with the spot just under your eye."

– Edgar Allan Poe

CONTENTS

FOREWORD

Youssef Alaoui Fdili's short novel THE BLUE DEMON is a delightful paean to a bygone era. It is an arrow passing through the center of a drifting, splashing globe. Welcome to the age when men guide themselves by the merciful light of celestial bodies, keeping time not by the ticking of clocks but by the rhythmic lapping of waves.

As the novella begins, a questionable seaman wavers in the *mizzen nest*. The reader will become amply familiar with the significance of this object, as the writer returns to it as a point of reference amongst an otherwise kaleidoscopic sea of possibilities, most of them bearing a quite ominous nature. The protagonist remarks:

At first sight of the wretchedly blue, borderless horizon, my condition had set in.

This line signifies the beginning of a rapid wooing, if only the reader will summon the will to stand watch over this concentrated sea of a book, despite lingering Sartrean *Nausea.*

With a writing style clear, crisp and momentarily explosive, Alaoui describes how arms may *brace like pilings* and the reader is somehow transformed into the ship itself for a moment. Imagine that.

Another revisited theme would be the marvelously described ripples that sensuously slash the surface of the water with increasingly hectic regularity as the story progresses. The fictitious ripples mirror actual ripples that rise from within the depths of the subconscious of the reader over the course of this book. What is this subconscious leviathan that Alaoui tantalizes to our knowing scope? Is it something as simple as a "sea monster," or are there more psychically impressive machinations at play? Of course, the writer's use of the mechanism of "sea monster" is by no means banal. The descriptions of this natural aberration surpass the established literary tradition. Alaoui's "great white whale" is a psychedelically blossoming semiotic storehouse.

In *The Blue Demon*, Alaoui conjures a zygote that only the orgy of Herman Melville, H.P. Lovecraft and the Grim Reaper on morphine could accidentally on purpose sort of produce. This of course is a lovely pleasure of pregnancy for the reader to witness coming to full term and exploding from the inkwell womb of the writer.

The holy trinity is fractured; its ghost is scattered over the water. It is a monster and a sea and a ship and a frightened collection of men. The cult religion that is this book is born. The "talking in tongues" sounds much like:

VVVVZHGGHH… T U L I O …
ZZZZZJHHHVVV.

Would the reader be attracted to subtle phantasmagoria shifting into chaotic high-seas battles of man versus alien entity? If so, the reader could do no better in our common era than *The Blue Demon*, a guided meditation into a jolly and decisive madness that begins with a flash of nausea that bobs on an otherwise sweetly nautical nihilism.

The protagonist does not belong in this horizon-lined vacuum, speckled with aberrant sea foam. The reader, then, doesn't belong either, and yet already the low, throbbing chelations of the soul of the book, indeed the soul of the author, are destined to hypnotize you into an all too brief love affair with this subtly glamorized crew of Spaniard salty dogs that only a Lovecraftian mother could love, though the reader will find the narrator places them at the perfect distance for non-Lovecraftian mothers to love, as well.

"Briefly stated," our protagonist is "Nickel," an enigmatic Moor with a mind well-populated with ideas and pertinent wisdom well-tailored to the setting of a wretched blue that is home to a psychotically omnipotent presence. The reader suspects that Nickel would be meditating on a game of blackjack had he his druthers though life, and our author, the Nickel-like arbiter god of this novella-sized life, finds him sorely out of place, a Muslim on a ship inhabited primarily by Catholic Spaniards, adrift on the infinitesimal rolling plain of the high sea. His glaring agoraphobia is the key that settles we readers into a desirous existential vertigo; being the only medicine for our own condition of uncertainty.

Alaoui knows that all of us, like Nickel, have our own debts to pay on dry land. With a wink and a naughty smile, he invites us on his voyage, his *descent into the maelstrom*, and graciously asks that the reader take no offense at how his book's loveliest jokes have severed heads as punch lines. Nickel's burgeoning affliction in the open blue fever dream of the wild waters could be an allegory for coping with modernity; the quest for identity and intellectual or spiritual freedom. Let us thumb our nose at modernity and enjoy this book; the corporeal turning of pages, the all-too-alive quality of weight resting in the hand waiting to become movies in the mind.

Alaoui is a tantalizing pusher-man, his crispy, dark chanticleer-pirate-of-the-morning voice leading you league after league out into the blue abyss of his and your own shared imagination. You are the reader, and excitement becomes you…

And once we have enlisted onto this voyage and the ceremonial bottle has shattered against the barnacle-graffitied hull and we are reading and reading and reading…

The open nature of the sea disarms, disorients. The mind opens to the adventure and the lyrical treasures of the author's arsenal-like language. Once land can no longer be seen, the novella, like the ship, is giddily inescapable. We could dive from the side of *The Blue Demon* though we would only find that the blue demon has become our environs.

The author, you, Nickel, God, the Blue Demon: we are all in this together now. There is nothing left but you, the Blue Demon, space and opportunity.

Alaoui enchants us in intimate space, the happy nightmare of the Blue Demon. He seizes the opportunity.

We are all in this together now. Read.

For the time it takes to traverse this tiny novel, I invite you to open your sails and allow the author to blow phantasmagoric smoke in your face. In the paradigm that blue demons inhabit, the smoke becomes the sweetest of salty sea winds, and off we go to read, to read, to read…

We are all in this together now.

The author disrobes. The sea disrobes. Nickel disrobes. The reader disrobes. The blue demon disrobes. We are all in this together now. We are complicit. Read!

(Bells ring – drums beat – singing bowls sing – you are shocked with the divine vitality of The Reader.)

– Dennis Ray Falcon Powell Jr.

I. PROLOGUE

High above the ship, tucked away in the mizzen nest, invisible to the others, did I confront my mortal enemy. Grappling the sides of the wretched bucket served no good. To steady my spasms, I dug my nails deep into the sides, yielding nothing but blood and splinters. My forehead drained down my face. My arms, braced like pilings, sent jolts of pain up to my neck. My stomach heaved. If only I had kept my eyes on the floor of the nest. At first sight of the wretchedly blue, borderless horizon, my condition had set in. It was only a matter of time before I would lose consciousness.

In an effort to save myself, I tried calling down to the others on deck. "Ehhuah!" My tongue had swollen and dried. "Eh - huaahg!" No response. My vision was going. By carefully wrapping one of the ropes around my arm, I was able to secure my shoulder with the intention of letting myself down securely, should I lose hold of the rigging. Instead, I misplaced my leg and spun about mid-air, with a blinding flash of pain, and fell head first toward the deck below.

II. THE HANGED MAN

"What's this guy's name again?"

"He's an Arab we hired on at the dock."

"What's his NAME, does anyone know?"

"Nicolas… Nickel… "

"That's no name for an Arab…"

"Nickel. Nickel! NICKEL! Can you hear me?"

I awoke below deck on the dining room table.

"He's opening his eyes. He'll be fine. Get him a nip of rum."

Briefly stated, my name, in Arabic, is Mukhtarr. In Spanish, Nicolas. On a ship, I prefer that people call me Nickel.

"What happened to you, boy? We had one hell of a time pulling you down from the mizzen. You were hanged upside-down by one leg! The tangle of ropes that snagged you actually saved your life when you fainted. But you'd have smashed your head against the mast had we not cut you free!" Handsley, the boatswain, put both hands down beside me on the table. An Englishman by birth, the seas had tanned his skin and he suffered from a permanent squint. He could command a crew or berate them with equal ease in Spanish, French, or English. He was fully invested in the men of his charge, and he had never seen me before.

"Th - thank you." I said, rising. "I assure you, I'm quite all right now." I stumbled, sliding off the table, trying to remove myself from the center of attention.

"Don't mention it. Now what happened up there?"

"It won't ever happen again." I said, stirring uncomfortably. He gave me a stern look.

"What happened? Are you fit to work?"

"Quite all right, sir. I assure you."

"Well. We need every hand ready and able. I can't have you dropping unconscious while you're on duty. If there's something I need to know then let's have out with it!"

"How soon do we get to the next port?"

He looked at me shrewdly. We had barely left the harbor. "We're due in two weeks. Why?"

"Oh, okay. Sir, I'd rather not keep watch from the mizzen nest."

The boatswain's eyes screwed up a bit.

"I've only done that once before, for a couple weeks, right, and only on the Mediterranean. This is a whole new game…"

He leaned over the table at me.

"Er, I'd rather work in the galley."

He jumped. "Helping the cook?"

"Mopping, cleaning, below…" I gestured around us. "That's what I'm good at."

He was moon-eyed. "But you signed up for mizzen!"

"That is what they told me I would do."

"Who signed you on?"

I looked down. I was practically a castaway, on a Dutch pinnace called The Ladybird, crewed by Spaniards, most knowing one another from previous voyages, headed for trade in the Caribbean Sea. I owed a great gambling debt in Seville due to my personal compulsions. The only way out was to jump a packet down the river, make haste to Gibraltar, and sign on with the first ship headed out. My hope was, aside from being forcibly away from games of chance and the casino thugs, to earn back my sum and repay it upon return.

"How did you get here!" he pounded his fist on the table.

"I signed up at the port. I'm sorry but I don't remember seeing you there. I think the captain had already boarded. Yes. I remember now. You were also aboard, operations were underway, there was a situation near mizzen. Because my gaze was in that direction at the time, the man just pointed at me and told me to board. I was signed right on, ran up to the mizzen mast and started helping."

"Fer chrissake…"

"Why?"

"Well yes we needed the help, but you should have told someone."

"What?"

"What you do. What you're good at…"

"Um." Okay, now I should tell him. This is as good a time as any.

"What!" he said, looking me dead in the eye.

"I'm actually…"

"Actually what?"

The others leaned in.

"I'm actually physically ill when I see the open sea."

"You WHAT? You are a sailor aren't you?"

"When I need to be."

"And what does that mean?"

"It means that, yes, I … I have a touch of the nerves. Wide open spaces affect me."

"Then why, sir, have you chosen to work on ships for a living?"

A few were chuckling.

"Because it's the best way I know to earn money for a time without spending it."

"Fair enough. But how do you survive on a ship at sea? Tell me that."

"I work in the galley. And I can also stand night watch when everyone else needs to sleep." That statement seemed to meet with no small amount of satisfaction. A few grunts emanated.

"Very well. So a dark sea doesn't affect your… illness?"

"Not in the least. I can see well in the dark, I don't need much sleep, and if there's any disturbance I am immediately responsive."

"And storms?"

"No problem. I am as sure-footed as they come."

"Sounds all right then. We'll start you working the mizzen by night right away and then switch you to watch as the need arises."

"Thank you, sir."

"Anything else?"

"Well, I'm best in the galley during the day so I don't have trouble stopping for prayers."

"Stopping for prayers?"

"I pray three times briefly during work shifts if my job allows."

"You're a Mohammedan."

"Yes sir."

"What are you doing in Spain?"

"What is anyone doing in Spain? I'm making a living. The war ended hundreds of years ago."

Silence. There was not a Muslim in the lot.

"After all, we taught your people seafaring," I added.

Handsley folded his arms. "Is that so. Well we taught your people shipbuilding."

"Well, that could be said… but I–"

"SHHHT!" another, Samuel, interrupted us with an emotive glare in his face. "There's a storm…"

"A big one," said someone else, looking around him, as if to reckon its direction.

Sure enough, beyond the normal sounds of the sea, was a whine. It sounded like the churning of a windmill grindstone against a rusty metal plate. It was a cyclone approaching from the Southeast. We looked at one another. I saw the boatswain listening, calculating.

Then he spoke: "It will be on us in less than a day. It is probably tightening. We'll need every hand available to lower all masts and secure every sail, chain, shank, and every last god-damned bauble on this ship. I want the sails folded and bound triple-tight at the base of each mast. Anything that you do not want to cave in your skull has got to be bound triple-tight. Once this ship starts rocking I want the base of each mast to be padded well enough so that when our bodies are rendered into projectiles we can spare as many shattered limbs as possible. From the depth of the whine, I'm gauging the cyclone won't be over in a day either. So practice your grip, mates, because we'll need to be nimble as lemurs for the next three days. Someone wake the captain!"

"The captain is awake," stated the captain, stepping down into the lounge. He was a man a bit taller than most, strong in the shoulders, dark in the face. The captain's concerns were the owners of the ship, the transport company, and shipping logistics. He looked like he'd been through his share of troubles and now, in his later years, kept mostly to himself and the first mate. He had worked with both the first mate and the boatswain before. He had full confidence in Handsley. The boatswain was captain of the crew, and was known to have given the captain's orders before he'd made them known, but there was no doubt who ran the ship. For better or worse, the captain conducted operations from his quarters, relying on the first mate and capable Handsley to carry it all out. When addressed with his given name, which only few could do, I heard they called the captain *Tulio*. "Boatswain, you will have the crew furl all sails and tie them to the base of the masts."

"Done sir!"

"Please advise the carpenters to ready their tools in case they are needed."

One of the carpenters was among us.

"Ready your tools!" the boatswain looked over his shoulder at him.

"Ready!" was the reply.

The captain cut in again, sharply. "Make sure your tools are set properly in their boxes and *pegged* so the saw won't fly up at you when you need it!"

"Understood."

"Go now!" said the captain directly to the carpenter, still sitting. "Boatswain, come with me. The rest of you have your orders. Please rouse the rest of the crew and GET-TO-IT!"

It was done. I went on deck with the others. I climbed the mizzen and furled the sails with my team. We had neatly folded and bound every sail triple-tight at the base of our mast in short time. As we worked, and perhaps because we were attuned to it, the static whine grew ever more apparent. This was the oncoming storm. It sent out vicious waves before it, clipping our backside, as if to sweep the ocean clean for its appearance.

I managed to tidy things up in the mizzen nest as best I could. I covered the area with a tarp stretched all around the sides, tight like a drum. The height doesn't bother me. It's the clear blue sky and a flat sea that makes me nervous. If I don't have a context, or if the night is very dark, then my space-sickness won't bother me. In fact I prefer to work in as dim a light as possible, particularly starlight.

I can spot rocks in the blackest night from the way the water's surface breaks up the starlight. I imagine I can see rocks straight down through the mass of water, hanging like limpid blobs. I tell myself I can see them. Sometimes, I tell others I see them.

Once we finished, dawn broke. Handsley had most of us go down and hang in our bunks. We chatted, smoked, slept. I slept a good long time.

III. THE CYCLONE

Someone came to my bunk and woke me. "Nickel. Get up. Handsley's got you on galley. Like you wanted. You're on as soon as you can get there." I looked around. It was twilight.

"Did I sleep all day? I wanted galley after noon. I can keep watch at night."

He shook his head. "It is still day. The storm has blackened the sky."

The confinement of the galley was a pleasure. A narrow hallway it was, really. The high winds hadn't come upon us yet, but vicious waves were kicking up now and again. I could see why I was needed so urgently. One of the waves had knocked a pot of stew down the wall, behind the stove.

The cooks, Royas and Alejandro, had left it for me to clean up. Shortly after, I went on deck to help secure the last stitches of rigging. The skies were dark by four. The waves bashed us with greater force and regularity. Visibility to the Southeast decreased to a purple fuzz as the squalls converged upon us. My watch began at six.

A narrow band of white remained to the North. I could see placid weather in the distance. It was a vision as distant as an imaginary fairyland with sunbeams dancing on the water, illuminating a volley of bouncy white clouds. It was a squashed children's diorama.

I had never heard of, much less seen a ship with all its rigging stowed. The captain's method was quite his own. Our denuded masts resembled a burned-out forest. I tested the captain's padded mast strategy. They were still stout, but wouldn't crack your head on impact. Aside from the increasing high waves, we were still good until seven.

Dinner was served below. They brought me a bowl. The rains started at eight. Winds kicked up very heavy soon after. I struggled to hang on. They brought me to my bunk at ten, once they saw my condition. I would have stayed out there if needed, but two others took my place, the helm was secured, and it was decided that we should drop anchor to maintain stability.

All the ballast had been moved to dead center and our heaviest boxes fore and aft. I slid out of my wet clothes and into my bunk. My hammock rocked with the ship. I imagined I was perfectly stable and that the ship moved about independently of me. I was tired of cold salt water. I tried to sleep.

I must have been asleep, because I awoke on the floor rolling into a bulkhead. Voices were yelling. We were listing badly. We had lost everyone on deck. A few bumps and bruises on the lower decks, but the rest of us held on with all our might.

Handsley was picking his way through diagonal beams, yelling over all others; "Tighten every God-damned latch, bolt and porthole in your immediate vicinity!"

I heard the captain's voice booming elsewhere; "Casas!" A deckhand. "I mean it! Over there! What does that look like!"

Some were regaining consciousness and others were nursing limbs. It was difficult to move about, as the ship flopped in varying degrees of sideways. I found my boots in the flotsam and put them on. I found someone else's pants, better than mine, in a locker, and a shirt and hat and coat, and put them all on. "Sir!" I said to the boatswain as he approached.

"Nickel!"

"What can I do!"

"Very troubling news. We lost the first mate and some of the patrol. If you can, make your way to every point below and assess the damage. I'd be much obliged."

"And above deck?"

"We're as sealed in as possible from the upper deck. We're going to let the storm take us where it will and figure that out when it's over. We believe we'll only have four more hours of this as the eye passes us!"

"Sealed?"

"Sealed!" He smiled. I examined it as I walked around. They had nailed every door shut with a tarp in it and tarped up every window as well. I was to check as much of the interior of the ship as I could for leaks or standing water. Yet, fording a tilted ship is no small task. The crew, now eighteen men, were all fine. They were in the process of securing everything the storm had chucked off its perch, kicking their way through a soup made of rank seawater and debris. I was ready for someone to point out that I was wearing his hat or coat, but no one seemed concerned, all were adequately dressed.

When I descended into the hold, I found some boxes had shifted. I fetched a hammer, nails and a length of rope. Better than nails, I found iron spikes. There were already pegs for rope, but spikes would allow me to secure the boxes by hammering my knots into the beams. A set of pulleys in the hold made it easy to hook one box at a time and center them. As I was standing between two piles of boxes with my arms outstretched, a wave threw me down with the boxes landing over me. I was knocked out cold.

A day later someone came down and found me. It was De Las Casas. I was deeply pinned.

"Nickel!"

"Wuh."

He was laughing in relief to have found me living. "We thought we had lost you!"

I noticed the ship was upright.

IV. THE KELP FIELDS

Casas pulled the boxes away from my chest and shoulders. "We have Handsley, the captain, and thirteen of the crew. You'll see. We thought for sure you had somehow been thrown over… how did you end up down here?"

"The boxes…"

"Okay, let me help you up. Did you come down here on the first day of the storm, or were you here the whole time?"

"Handsley sent me…"

"Okay, okay I'll ask… Oh, man! Can you use your arms?"

"Hurts."

"Okay well can you stand up? Wow, it smells like you might have pissed your pants! Ha–ha! Sorry. Damn, how long have you been down here?"

Casas managed to walk me out to the nearest bunk. I stayed there for three days. They brought me soup. I learned that six others were convalescing on the level above, with varying minor bone fractures and sprains. I counted my blessings. I had bruised my collarbone and sprained my shoulders pretty badly but my legs were fine. I just needed rest. The kitchen was functioning, the hull was sound. We lost the mizzen mast in the second half of the storm. Good riddance. We had been blown a great distance to the North. Even with every sail stretched to maximum, we were barely crawling; partly due to a lack of wind, but mostly due to the nature of the water.

The sea temperature had increased and was thick with raspy, grabbing branches of kelp. The kelp webbing was directly beneath us and as far out as we could see in every direction. It grew so knotted and vast that in places branches mounded up on one another and decayed in the sun, giving rise to secondary and tertiary growths that stretched on and on, resembling not just open fields, but land masses and mountains. They looked like islands with trees and rocks, but it was just kelp and rotted kelp and more growths borne upon that. We were clearly stranded, with no exit in sight.

Antonio, the only other man from the mizzen team, came to visit me one day in my bunk. "Do you think you can start your night watch?"

"Certainly. I'm no champ on the rigging. If I'm called to hoist or lower a sail in a hurry, you'd be better off with another man."

"No worries there, friend. We haven't needed to move the sails in four days."

"Of course. Then I'll be ready. When am I on?"

"I'll let the boatswain know. He'll probably have you on at about nine tonight, if you're able," I nodded. "Good. That will cover us until first light. Glad you're feeling better. By the way, José is angry that you messed up his nice breeches! We found your trunk with your own things in it. It's upstairs."

José, it turned out, had come to sailing from a moderately wealthy background. Well he can keep his nice trousers. Thank God I can wear my own hat and coat too, I thought. I remembered some tobacco, in the pocket of my coat, and wondered if it was up in my trunk as well. My hips were still creaky but I could navigate the stairs just fine, especially, because the waters were dead calm.

Something else I noticed on that day; big, fat, loathsome, lazy, flies. The air and waters were so stagnant that, even though we were miles at sea, there was enough rotted material around us to have birthed a race of heavy-moving and complacent flies. They must be feasting on carrion trapped in the kelp entanglements.

My first few nights of watch were absolutely uneventful, which gave my body the time it needed to heal. We could see and even hear tremendous black squalls inching along the horizon to the South; much like the one we rode in on. The crew, although less than half who started, moved about their tasks like automatons. The rituals of keeping the decks clean, tending to the masts and sails, then retreating below deck for food and rest, rendered us no more than figurines on a clock; moving out one hole, dancing a bit in the middle, then swinging about the wheel into the other hole. The captain was bound to introduce a plan. I figured a week or so of banality could be a part of his plan, allowing us to rebuild our strength and our senses.

V. NIGHT WATCH

But the warm days and gelatinous waters had a way of wearing down our senses. We began to doubt our perceptions. At night, as I smoked, I could see the kelp slowly moving with the current. I remembered how Royas and Alejandro had pulled up some water one day, as there had been a debate about its viscosity. We had been mopping with seawater regularly but we passed a spot that could have been mistaken for aspic. It appeared sufficiently spiced, dark and quivering. They threw it out on the deck. The water was full of kelp and fish eggs. These were rich hatcheries here. We would not go hungry, but at this rate, we would not go home soon either.

Now, on deck by myself, I realized that I had been seeing defined shapes swirling in the water. Something of great size swept by us, creating odd ripples that forced my attention upon them. Wide bellies erupted from the spicy mass and spread across the surface. It couldn't have been due to standing rocks. The wind, of course, was next to flat and the current only slightly nudging. But these eruptions, although subtle, were unmistakably focused about the ship. I imagined a tremendous thinking being; suckling and perceiving our presence, noting our solitude, our wayward direction. I imagined it was aware of our predicament and that it desired to be close to us, that it desired us to be within it. The eruptions subsided in a few minutes. I discounted the event as only one of several phenomena we had already encountered. After all, this was the sea: engenderer of all phenomena, including humanity.

VI. BOLAS!

I finished my shift and slept soundly without incident. I dreamt of women and their bodies. The sea was a body and desired us to be within her. I was on my way to conjoin with the sea when I was rousted from my bunk for duty. I took my late noon breakfast consisting of the usual biscuit and eggs but today they were spiked with kelp and other sea goodies Alejandro had scrounged with his basket-on-a-rope.

I served my time cleaning and arranging the galley, as I preferred, then night watch, as the others supped and made their way to their bunks. The captain had revealed his plan. We were to take shifts and row due south, to a current that would lead us to land. No one on board looked forward to this. We had lavished on stolen time here in the doldrums.

That night, again, I noticed odd movements of the sea. This became alarming not quickly, but slowly, as I watched the surface heave and then break apart, not revealing a grand fish or fin. Then, I could swear my legs perceived a vibration from the walls of the craft, transferred to the decks. Something had touched the ship! But it was not a rock. Something long and soft, but substantial. Thick strands of kelp, perhaps. Again it happened. I imagined the sea gently licking the sides of the ship. Ah, she was tasting us. And then, a nudge! The ship heaved to port and then righted. "Captain!" A few people raised their voices in alarm.

"What's going on!" a tired Handsley stood at his door, buckling his trousers and straightening his cap. "Dammit, Nickel, what the devil is going on here!" we both ran to the captain's quarters and banged on the door. He was up and aware and needed a minute to put himself together. The crew was getting up and asking each other questions. As we hurried back to the deck and found it absolutely calm, we began looking over the sides. Suddenly, the ship lurched again. Most of the crew were thrown off balance. "Slub-bub-bah H E LP !"

"Blood of God!" someone cried from aft. It was Marques. He swore he watched a man named Bolas rise from his side, lift upright, and drift, flailing, over the rails, with both arms and legs moving in empty air.

"You mean he fell over the railings," said Handsley, sternly.

"No – No! It didn't happen like that! You heard him! You must have heard him yell for help! But there wasn't any time!"

"To help him from sliding over the railings when the ship lurched!"

"No! My God! He was already down! I mean, we were all flattened on the deck just now…"

"What's happened?" said the captain.

Handsley explained. "Bolas went over the side."

Marques' eyes were adamant. He brought his fists up to his chest. "He was picked up and taken!"

"Somehow, he managed to slip over the railings when we hit the second rock," said Handsley. Just then the ship creaked as if something were squeezing it.

"What in God's name!" cried the captain. He turned to me and said: "Cricket!"

"Nickel" said Handsley.

"Nickel! Please. Try to see if we are hitting rocks or land or whatever it is."

"Yes sir!" with that, I headed off to the dark side of the ship; the bow, where Bolas had slipped off. At the stern, Handsley and the others were calling for Bolas in case he was still within earshot.

The captain ordered the skiff to be lowered and they set out on the water with lanterns held high, calling for Bolas. I saw no rocks beneath us. I saw nothing but soft, spongy, knotted, swaying, despicable, drifting kelp. Nothing. I sighed. That was it.

"Boatswain, there are no rocks near us. I'm surprised we're moving at all because the kelp is so thick, but certainly, there are no rocks. I can maintain watch until daybreak. I'll of course let you know if anything else happens."

"Of course. That will be fine. Thank you, Nickel." they wrapped up their search below and they all turned in, muttering. One might think Bolas was just tucked away in the poop, but he was indeed gone, and that was the only result of the amazing incident that was certain. The rest of it could have just been a flight of my imagination, if everyone else on board hadn't felt it too.

I smoked and stood out on my watch, looking for ruptures on the water's surface, but nothing emerged. Nothing happened. Daylight brought more warmth and more dead air. We were practically aground.

VII. A GHOST HAS TAKEN THEM

Next day, the captain exclaimed we would escape these waters or perish trying. We dug up some oars from the hold and hung them out the windows. We put the skiff in front and set six men in it rowing with all their might. When I got up, all was in place and there was talk of the men experiencing what they called "lumps" in the water that slowed progress, but they went right on rowing. Oars out the windows, even extended with spare lumber, proved ineffective. The sails were taken down because the wind had been pushing us north. Apparently the current would eventually place us back where we had started, but not without moving us to open sea first. Sadly, it would take us a year to complete the cycle. The teams understood and paddled themselves silly all through the day, due south, to catch the captain's current. At evening, they brought up the skiff and the oars. The men were beat. We would try a new team in the morning.

At dinner, someone heard a voice from down in the water.

"It's Bolas!" said Marques.

"How could he –" said Casas.

"Sh - sh - shhh…"

"I don't hear anything. We just rowed all day…" said Antonio.

We ran to the deck to listen. The flies were all about us.

Somewhere in the dark we heard: "Zzz - ghk - sss"

"Uh, that's probably an air pocket in a pile of rotted plants," said Casas.

Antonio looked at Marques. "Yeah! It's rotten gas like in your head, you idiot!" Handsley had come up and was listening intently. "Shht!"

"Sssszzzmmmzzzzghhhzzzzmmmvvvvvv… Gollasss."

"Bolas?" whined Marques.

"SSSBOLAS."

"My god!" cried Handsley. Get him some rope, someone, Blancas! Get him some rope man, and step to it! We have a man overboard!" Blancas was nearest to a good pile of rope. He started letting it over the side frantically. "Bolas! Grab this rope! Can you see the rope?"

"Golusss" was all we heard from the water. I saw movement and said "Over there!" and they shined their lanterns in the new direction but we only perceived a deep swirling among the plants.

"GYAAAAAAGH!"

We swung around with the lights and saw Blancas moving up sideways, not in control of his body, up and over the railings. It must have been a trick of the eye or the moving lights, but I noticed his jacket rippling over his midriff as if affected by a great wind. Then he descended silently into the water.

"Blancas! God damn it Blancas! What the hell are you doing!" yelled Handsley.

"We've lost him." I said.

"Nonsense!" said the boatswain. "He's just tangled up in some of that rope. We'll pull him up quick. You and Alejandro go drag up the rope! He's caught by the leg, surely, so be careful!" we went to pick up the rope and there was no weight to it. Blancas was gone. We pulled up the entire soggy rope. Apart from a few weeds it was free of anything. No sign of him. The water was completely calm. The night was absolutely silent. Handsley and the captain looked at one another.

I sobbed once, uncontrollably. Someone at the back of the ship called for Bolas again. "Enough!" yelled the boatswain. The rest of the crew came up to our huddle at the bow. "Now we've lost Blancas as well," said the captain. "We have to continue to make our way out of here tomorrow. I can't stand to keep losing men in calm waters."

We extinguished the lanterns and made ready for another push in the morning. I was to keep watch until daybreak, but the boatswain gave me two companions; Juan Carlos the carpenter and a young sailor named Salvador, whom we called Salvo. Nothing else happened that night. We rotated stations periodically; fore, aft, amidships.

Despite our efforts, not much happened the next day either. The captain had the skiff go out before us, but the kelp was so tangled, they could barely chop a path for us to float through. They lost a lot of sweat and didn't make much of a dent in the weed.

Night watch started again in the new way. Salvo, it turned out, was cousin to Bolas. "This crap is so thick he coulda stepped right up outta that water and stood on a heap until we swung around! The captain shoulda stayed put. Man Bolas was a good guy. He got me this job!" we were chatting a while because the night was so still.

Juan Carlos replied. "You don't know. He could have been unconscious."

"Everybody heard him yell. You don't yell when you're unconscious!"

"He yelled when he saw he was going to hit his head. Then he fell over silent."

"That's just it! On a still night?"

"The ship had tipped! He might have lost his footing."

"Nobody saw him fall. And yet he went overboard. Nobody trips and falls like that. Certainly not Bolas. Not even drunk."

"Right… well, how'd he go over? Maybe he jumped. It's been so bloody boring in these doldrums, he might have." said Juan Carlos.

"Jumped? Are you out of your mind? What do you know. You're just a contracted carpenter. He's been on a million boring trips, hell, most of them are boring! That's what makes a great trip! As boring as possible! I want to be on the voyage where nothing happens! Then I'm sure to come back alive and with good pay!"

"I know about pay, you runt…"

"C'mon now," I said, "let's get to the watch and–"

"Say Nickel," said Salvo.

"What."

"You've got a great excuse to not get in the skiff like the rest of us. You're down there, in the kitchen, mopping up and sharpening knives for the cook."

"I'm sharpening the knives for your neck!" I said to the teen, a false threat. He scoffed.

"Hell I'll just run out on deck in broad daylight! You'll never catch me!"

"Don't make fun of him Salvo. You don't know what it's like. Nickel. Maybe you could try to row tomorrow. Think up a way. I don't know, you could throw a sack over your head or something and get out there to show the rest of the crew you don't think you're special. You know."

He had a point. "I'm aware of that. I…"

"Ha–ha! That's hilarious! Put ol' Nickel out there in the skiff with a sack on his head! He'll choke on his sweat! And he'll look like such a–"

"SALVO!" we both said, turning to him.

"The boy is right. That's why I won't be wearing a sack. But if I could make myself a mask to reduce my vision it would be like going out on a very foggy day."

"God-damn we could use a bit of fog. I have sweat blisters in my sweat blisters," said Juan Carlos.

"And I've got blood blisters in my blood blisters! Let's get him out there tomorrow!" said Salvo. It was agreed. We split up and took our watch for the rest of the night.

VIII. NICKEL HELPS OUT

"Sir," I said, addressing Handsley. "I would like to row the skiff today."

"Well we could certainly use the help, but, your… illness?"

"I have a method."

In less than a half hour I found myself making my way down to the little boat with a fresh team to relieve those who had been rowing since daybreak.

"How's it been?"

"Goopy and lumpy," was the reply. Hernandes, an ex-soldier, was stationed at the front, leaning over the prow with a cutlass. "I'm staying," he said. So he was to cut our way through as I, and three others, young Salvo, Alarcan– a student from Valencia, and a large, brutish sailor named Montoya, took up the oars. I had fashioned a white bandage for my eyes out of a shirt. It let just enough light through for me to recognize shapes. It still made me uneasy to be stuck in such a small craft on the open sea. I tightened my mask in case it should slip. I touched either shoulder and asked Allah to protect me. Hernandes and Montoya made the sign of the cross.

"HA! That ain't gonna help!"

"Shut up and show some respect, Salvo!" said Hernandes as he raised his sword.

We all drank water and urinated on our hands to keep the blisters down. Then we rowed. Hernandes chopped and chopped, from side to side, over the front of the boat, with his knees nestled into the prow. As I pulled, I noted the textures of the passing webwork. It felt possible to reach my oar down into the morass, then dig at the side of a branch and use it to propel us forward. The water occasionally came at us in twisting lateral waves that would pass under the boat and lift us up, over, and down the other side. But were these branches somehow articulated? Were they anchored deep at the bottom of the sea and so massive that they lifted our little boat as we passed them? "Lumps?" I said out loud.

"Yes!" said Hernandes from his sword-prayer perch, "these are lumps! They're pesky as hell and I can't chop deep enough to get them! They seem to come at the boat from all possible angles!"

"It – it doesn't make sense," I muttered. I continued to row. The kelp was thick-stemmed and hollow, with giant pods. The worst were shaped like bullwhips and seemed interminably long. This I knew from watching at night. Then my oar hit a real "lump" that was noticeably fatter. My forehead had soaked my mask completely. It itched, and as I reached my hand up to adjust it, I decided to take a tiny peek into the water to see if I could identify the structure of this tremendous weed lolling under our boat. What I saw was ghastly. It was not a weed. It moved of its own volition. It was a tentacle; colored blue like the sky, but the skin tones moved in ripples like the surface of the water. To anyone else but me, it might have been perfectly camouflaged; invisible. But I was quite sure that I saw companion tentacles reaching from the same direction, following our tiny craft, studying it, playing with it, moving around the efforts of our oars. I saw it all in an instant. My body froze. I screamed. My crew-mates saw me lifting my mask.

"Nickel took his mask off!"

"Get your mask on!"

I shook uncontrollably. They pulled us back up to the ship.

"Get him on board!"

"What happened to Nickel!" said Handsley. They explained and took me, wobbly, back to my bunk.

"He lifted his mask. Why the hell did you lift your mask, Nickel?"

"I – I was hot. I thought it would be okay, just for a bit." I didn't dare tell them what I had seen under the water. They would never believe me. They would be right not to. It could have just been my nerves. I couldn't risk it. If I was right, or if they believed me, it would cause chaos onboard, especially since we were quite trapped among the weeds.

IX. THE VISITOR RETURNS

I lay in my bed until after sundown. Then I took my post with Juan Carlos. Antonio from the mizzen team substituted for young Salvador, who needed the rest. Antonio and Juan Carlos were already stationed at the fore and aft when I got on.

"Antonio!"

"How are you doing, Nickel! Better?"

We made our way toward one another at the bow when we heard Juan Carlos gasp and come running. "Oh sweet mother of God in heaven! Oh God! Oh my God please help me!" His eyes were wide with fright. "I've just seen the ghost of Blancas! I swear it!"

"Settle down and have a seat here," I said. Antonio put his hand down on Juan Carlos' shoulder.

"I swear it! His head rose up and turned to me! But he had no eyes! He was dead… so dead.

His face was mostly skull. It looked like he was trying to speak to me, but all he could say was 'Gol-usss' … oh my God I can't even make that noise myself because it scares me so!"

"No such thing as ghosts," said Antonio, flatly.

"Not now." I said.

"No. Really. I'm trying to help him. We're all on edge after losing our mates. Any one of us can reach the breaking point without much provocation." He had a good point. Then he continued. "Do you think you could have seen the moon?"

"No."

"A reflection of the moon?"

"No. Look around you. Is there a moon tonight? No. Besides, Blancas' head floated up out of the water in a swarm of flies! It hovered and then it turned to face me. Then it called, well, it seemed to be… asking for Bolas! Come on with me. I will show you, if it's still there. The mouth opened like it was going to speak, but the jaw dropped widely open. Too wide! Like he couldn't help it."

We went back to where he had seen the apparition. Then I said "Go stand right where you were before. Think about what you were doing at the time."

"I was leaning up against the railing, like so."

"Okay, now shhht. Just go back to your business and we'll stand back. Antonio! Look over his shoulder from starboard and I'll stay here. Everyone stay within sight of one another, and – stay – quiet."

"… here ghostie ghostie!" snickered Antonio.

"Shhht!" I was looking over Juan Carlos' head and at the sky behind him, shifting from side to side to see if there wasn't a rope with a knot that might have drifted into his peripheral vision. Nothing suspicious. I looked at Antonio smiling and shaking his head. Juan Carlos looked about himself nervously. There were a few more flies than usual. I watched them cavort on the beams. After about twenty minutes of waiting, Antonio's disposition relaxed. He lit his pipe. I felt sleepy.

Then we heard buzzing near the water: "Zzzz-mmmm-mmvvvvvvvghvvvv…" and then "Bolassss." We jumped. "Ahhhntonnnio." My heart just about leapt out of my chest. I motioned to the others to keep their places, but Antonio was very uneasy. Then I saw it. Amid a swarm of flies, a fat, oily, rippling tentacle, perfectly matching the night sky, rose up close to Juan Carlos, still standing nearest to the edge, with the head of Blancas piked at the tip like a hand puppet. The jaws of the rotted head moved sloppily. Flies poured out of the eye sockets. "Ahhhntoonnnio…" As it approached, Juan Carlos, who turned to face it, lost all sanity in an instant. He gasped and then ran below at top speed, with Antonio close behind.

I had unwittingly pressed myself between a stack of rope and the tool shed. I was completely ensconced in the dark. I watched the head bobble on the railing of the ship and then splash into the water. It was suddenly clear to me. The sea did want us inside it. This creature was oddly using the head as a piece of bait to lure us into grappling distance. It seemed to be attempting to speak by means of squishing pockets of air about its body, and worst of all, it was not only aware of us, but it had been stalking us, toying with us.

I entered the lounge to find the entire crew clustered around Antonio and Juan Carlos, who were wide-eyed and pale, each of them stammering about their story in sheer frenzy. "Nickel! Where have you been! What the hell happened up there? Where were you?" I had only been above for two or three minutes after the others.

"It's trying to speak."

"Is that what that sound, that wretched gurgling, is? That was a real ghost, right? Now you've seen it too!" said Juan Carlos, making the sign of the cross on his chest, kissing his thumb.

"Mother of God!" said Antonio, "What in Jesus' name is going on? Is this not the ghost of Blancas? We must have it exorcised from the ship!"

"God help us," said Marques.

"No need," I said.

X. EXPLANATION – AND A PLAN

"What do you mean?" said Juan Carlos, "We can't have the dead trying to climb aboard the ship… What can we do?"

The captain smoked his pipe, almost smiling. Handsley spoke up. "We need men on watch now more than ever. Who is willing to take shifts?" Casas raised his hand, then Salvo, then Royas. "One, two, three, we'll need six, maybe, to start." He looked at me. I nodded. Then, a grunt from Montoya and a defiant rise of the fist from Hernandes.

"May I please mention something here," I said.

"Nickel. Of course. What can you relate to us of your account?"

I drew a deep breath. "What we are facing is by no means a ghost." Grunts of denial emerged from the group. Sailors fancy tales of the supernatural. I continued. "Not at all. I'm afraid it's worse than that. As best I can figure, we are being pestered by a creature."

"A creature that just happens to look like dead Blancas?" interjected Juan Carlos. A few chuckles emanated.

"In a sense. I'm not certain if it is an octopus, but it is a highly intelligent, tentacled, sea creature; capable of mimicking our voices."

Groans of disapproval and disagreement, eye-rolling and thigh-slapping came from the crew.

"Of mimicking our voices!" I raised my voice, insistent.

"Hear him out! Maybe it's a phantom and maybe it's a giant sea creature. Just let me hear his ideas!" said Handsley.

"Of course it's trying to mimic our voices!" I said. "It only gurgles out –what–? Names that we have called out over the water! It follows our ship day and night! Tentacled animals are the cleverest of the sea! I believe this creature is fascinated with us. It can hear us speaking from under water. Imagine if you would, for a moment; it has never encountered a thing like us in its life span. Here it lives, in an infinite and extremely dense kelp forest, with nothing but fishes, eggs and crustaceans. Then all of a sudden, our wooden craft with a multitude of babbling, finless, hairy, air-breathing creatures crawling all over it, appears in its domain. It is the top animal here and we, the newcomers, are its ultimate topic of fascination!"

"How… utterly… bizarre," said Antonio. "And how do you know this?"

"Only by conjecture. For the most part."

"A clever squid you are!" said Salvo, winning laughter from the crowd.

"We don't know that it is a squid," I said in earnest.

"But it is plausible," said the captain. "Where there is plenty of food, and a giant undisturbed domain, giant creatures will dwell. Nickel. How do you figure it is a tentacled creature?"

"At first, it was a just a feeling that I quickly ignored. The ship had lurched. Most of you will remember that from a few nights ago. From below I'm sure it felt as if we had run into something. But from the topsides, from my watch, the sensation was more like our ship was being stroked along its hull. Then, in the skiff while rowing, I understood that the crew were describing 'lumps' in the water that caused the boat to bob."

"What of the lumps?" said Hernandes.

"It's studying us. It's toying with the skiff as we row. I noticed rolls on the water's surface coming at us from –lateral– directions. Once they encountered the boat, they had more the effect of a solid material; unlike the kelp that passed under us from front-to-rear as you chopped."

"And so you screamed." he said.

"No. And so I raised my mask."

"And your sickness got the best of you!"

"No. I –saw– a giant tentacle stroking the hull of the skiff!" A few grunted in disbelief. "It is true, I tell you. I'm good at distinguishing shapes in the water. I know."

"It was kelp! Nothing but kelp!"

"I saw the skin of the tentacle rippling in blue. All tentacled animals use rippling camouflage to match the water's texture! In fact I had seen it before, but held my tongue because I thought it a trick of the light."

"When?" said Casas.

"When Bolas was taken."

"How do you mean," said Marques.

"I noticed his shirt rippling wildly over his midriff. On a calm night. Like every night."

"His shirt rippling?" said Handsley.

"The creature's tentacle matched Bolas' shirt exactly, but kept the effect of moving water. Out of the water, it looked like wind."

"So we thought he had slipped overboard…" said Handsley.

"…When he was actually taken up and over the side by a disguised tentacle," said the captain. "Well I like this theory better than phantoms.

I've heard that octopi are masters of disguise. And what then is your explanation of the floating head?"

"It is nothing more than the actual head of our dear departed crew-mate, which this clever demon hoisted upon a tentacle in hopes that it would serve as a decoy, so that we might mistake it for one of our own."

"And… why *eat* us?" said Antonio.

"Yes! You say it is fascinated with us, so why not try to be our good-natured sea friend?" said Salvo, "and lead us on our way out of here?"

"Because, although it may attempt to mimic our voices, and it is clever enough to concoct a crude strategy, and has naturally camouflaged skin, this is still merely a creature we speak of. It has no greater functions than feeding, swimming, and reproducing."

"Perish the thought!" said Juan Carlos, "so you're saying there are more of these out here."

"For our sake, I'm hoping this one is the king of the realm," I said, "God willing."

"God save us," said Juan Carlos.

"If that *is* what this is," said the captain "then we must turn our attention to killing it before we can leave this place. It might actually be holding us back."

"Indeed…" said Handsley. "First, I would say, if anyone is assaulted with the head of Bolas or

Blancas, chop at it with your cutlass at the level of the railing. Since we are not able to spot the tentacle, viewing the head at the tip would give us a fair idea of how the tentacle is oriented. And no one on deck without his sword!" he said, looking around the room. "If you see something floating over the railing, calling out to you, you swipe at it – low! See if you don't hit some meat!"

"YEAH!" a good many chimed in.

"Now I cannot wait to see my cousin's face again!" cried Salvo. They pat him on the back.

The captain spoke to Handsley: "Have the next watch start now. Cutlasses in hand. Everyone else to bed. We'll need 'em rested for the morning. But, Handsley, I'll need to speak with you in my quarters."

Handsley turned to us and said, "first watch, now! Nickel, your team is through for the night. I need you three: Royas, Salvo, Hernandes. Get your swords. If you don't have a preferred one, grab one from the armory. Everyone else, arm yourselves, ready your weapons, keep them safely by your bunks and get some sleep before first call! If anyone sees anything, do not shout. Do not run, but quickly and quietly make your way down to meet the captain and myself in his drawing room. We need to learn about this event. As much as possible. If you are in trouble, remember: Chop low! Remember above all that we are still not certain what it is we are confronting. So I want us all to go about our business as normally as possible, but if you are startled by anything, please take note, because we need to study how each event forms, the circumstances, the minutiae, so to speak. Then we'll know what we're up against! Did I make myself clear!"

"YES – SIR!"

"Are there any questions about what to do the next time someone sees a head floating over the railing calling out your name?"

"NO – SIR!"

"And another thing before you go! Even if you so much as see an odd swirl in the water, take note. If you're bouncing up and down in the skiff, take note. We can all learn a bit from Nickel here on his attention to details!"

"YES – SIR!"

"Okay. Off with everyone. You grab your swords and get rested. Tomorrow will be pretty much like today. We can only hope. Except this time, we're paying attention! Good-night!"

"Good night sir, good night, Captain!" Grunts of *good night* and *good night sir* sounded from all around and everyone headed in different directions.

XI. BRIGHT DAYS

The following day was bright as a newly minted coin. I slept well and hard, feeling no small amount of satisfaction for having revealed my observations to the crew and even inspiring a plan of action, with their utter cooperation. Tales from the skiff were already circulating at the dining table as I took my place for breakfast.

"They're cutting every which way now!" said José, smiling.

"I'm cutting that thing to pieces," said Montoya. "I'll tie a sword to each forearm and just let that sorry creature try to get at me because I'll shred it like this and with one o' these!" The hulking Montoya moved his arms around the table in a jousting manner.

"Hey! Look out!" said José, perturbed.

The rest of us smiled, covering our plates from his wild swings.

"Really, though," Alarcan turned to me; "that thing has been throwing kelp across the skiff! Giant strands of it! We spend most of our time trying to untangle the skiff and the ship from more and more winding kelp!"

"The wretched thing is on to us!" said De Las Casas.

"Couldn't be…" I muttered.

"Why not," said Casas.

"Hm?"

"What you just said. It couldn't be? It's acting like it knows we mean to be rid of it! And why not, for killing our crew-mates, if the thing has any brains at all, it should know its days are numbered!"

"I'm gonna shred it!" said Montoya.

"What are the indications that the creature might be aware we intend to harm it?"

"Well for one, it's never slung kelp over the skiff before!" said Casas.

"M-hm"

"It seems to be trying to tie us back. To keep us here. Not just the skiff but the ship too. We had to swing to the rear of the ship to hack away strands that seemed deliberately wound around the rudder. It wasn't knotted but… it was wound around and around in spirals. We were back there for a good hour, just chopping, at daybreak this morning."

"Strange. I heard nothing… felt nothing. Did you?"

"No. I don't know how it happened, but we were pretty well fixed to the bottom. There's a good breeze picking up now so we should be outta this mess soon."

"You'll see how it is once you get out there. You're going out on the skiff again today, aren't you Nickel?" said Montoya.

"Of course…"

Handsley sat down with us. "I'm having extra crew surveil the perimeter of the ship. We think there may be more than one creature. They seem intent on holding us back." He put his hand to his forehead. "We'll never get out of here with these things conspiring against us. Alejandro, Casas, I want you to stand watch on either side of the aft decks. Take three guns a piece from the armory: Two rifles each and a revolver. Shoot them at the water at the earliest disturbance. If you see anything swirling, shoot it. Anything. If it's feeling around for us, then we will discourage it as best we can. No more hugging the ship for that wretched behemoth." Handsley smiled. "Okay?"

"Yes sir!" Casas and Alejandro were eager to plunder the firearms closet. "And our swords?"

"Whatever it takes. Make sure to bring down a hail of bullets once that pest nears the back end of the ship."

"As good as done, sir!" They took off smiling.

Handsley turned to Montoya and myself: "You two are scheduled to row on the skiff today. Nickel, are you ready? No fainting. I need you at your best. I'll have two men watching from the foredecks with rifles to cover you, but no more than five at a time in the skiff. It's mostly a game of chopping now. The wind is picking up. We'll soon be on our way."

"Will we have firearms, sir?" I asked.

"I can give you rifles but you'll be better off with swords at that distance."

I took my time to check every corner of the armory and came up with a slightly amusing old scimitar with a wider blade than those nasty little foils the others bandied about.

"Oh–HO!" They exclaimed as I descended into the skiff.

I'll admit that I was a bit of a sight with my baggy trousers cinched at the ankles, a wide-brimmed hat pulled low over my forehead, and my eyes masked off with a sheer white head-cloth. I brandished the scimitar in their direction.

"Woah–HO!" They raised their swords and oars in bravado.

No sooner had I taken my seat at the oar, when a giant wet vine of kelp flew across our mid-side, essentially pinning my knees, and those of Montoya, sitting to my left.

Montoya, without rising, quickly chopped us free. "How can you see in that get-up?"

I checked my blade and set it down to commence rowing. "I can see fine. Better than without it."

"But with that hat- how are you gonna see from above?"

"I'll worry about that."

"Look OUT!" said Montoya, now standing, to receive one of two large strands coming from opposite directions. The skiff took a dip. I chopped around me. José and Royas tore us free. The jostling drew rifle fire from the ship.

"Hey watch it!" yelled Royas.

The bullets fell well clear of us to either side. Samuel and Antonio grinned and waved down from the prow. Alarcan was hunched over the front of the skiff, knees embedded, chopping furiously at the weed. The waters were calm. The gunfire had somehow been effective.

"It's useless to row," I said. There was a wind, so we hoisted the sail to see if it would fill. "How many swords are here?"

Montoya gestured: "These two are mine."

"I have one," said Royas. "The best one!"

"Okay."

"I have just one," said José. "Were we supposed to bring more?"

"Well you never know."

"I have three. Here." said Alarcan.

"There you go! I'm going to try something. Let's use two of our oars and tie our swords to the back…"

"That's a waste of an oar!" José cut me off.

"It's a waste to row! Besides, we're dealing with something larger than a sword at arm's length here. I'm tying my sword to the end of my oar. You'll see."

"We must have a harpoon up in the ship," said Royas.

"Somewhere up there. Not down here." The waters gurgled around us. It drew more rifle fire from the ship. "Damn it!" I ducked.

"Quick! Tie these on me!" said Montoya, holding out his forearms. They were stout like thighs and scarred by rope and fishing tools. He grinned at me and nodded down to them, fists clenched. A strand of kelp smacked him over the head. He did not flinch.

"Allah-aqbar!" I said. Alarcan was up and on it, with José chopping behind him, clearing the deck of the skiff, throwing chunks overboard, tripping and stooping.

"Will you two quit monkeying around and get to work!" said José.

We ignored the remark. To humor Montoya, I pulled some rope, cut us a good length, tied the swords down as tightly as I could against his forearms, and then realized they'd go wobbly at the first thing he stabbed. He needed something flat to tie them down securely. "I'm not sure this will work."

"Why not! Why are you always trying to figure things out - watch!" and he brandished his swords about him, swinging into the air with alternate arms.

"Look out, man! Because! They'll fall off as soon as you use them. Let me see your shirt."

"Wha!"

"Take off your shirt. We'll cut the shirt into broad strips like this and tie the swords down flat on your forearms. Now that'll hold!"

"YES!" he smiled.

"I can hold my own swords," said José, shaking his head.

"You'll see. This will work great!" said Montoya. I carefully wrapped up his arms with the swords snugly fixed to the top of each fist. He grinned.

"Now how are we going to draw this thing up close enough for Montoya to stick his swords into it?" asked José.

"That…" I said, "is the best question I've heard all day."

XII. FIGHTING TENTACLES

Gunfire crackled from the back of the ship. "They're gone!" said José, pointing to where the two spotters had been standing on the prow.

"Let's pull the sail and get this thing around to the other side!" said Royas.

"Cut the line!" I said, as I cut my sword free from the oar.

No sooner had we rounded starboard than did we see the captain and Handsley, the latter pointing and shouting: "Get up on board! Do not go back there on the water! They're fighting the kelp from every which way! We need men and rifles on board right NOW!"

We scrambled topside and brought the swords. Montoya kept his attached to his forearms. "Montoya!" I yelled. In addition to the vines of kelp flying at the crew, who were struggling mightily to hack them back, I saw a mob of tentacles everywhere; feeling about the decks, opening and closing shutters and doors. Not only were tentacles keeping the crew over-occupied at the rear of the ship, but behind the lines of engagement, a completely independent investigation was being conducted. The monster was searching the ship. "Montoya wait! Come back!" He was running to fight the vines with the others. "Stop for a moment. Look there."

"Don't mess with me! We have to kill this son of a whore, now!"

"Take two seconds to cool down and look at that hatch."

"Yeah it opens when the ship moves. So what."

"But the ship isn't moving in a direction that might cause it to open. What do you think of that?"

"What?" Montoya put his hand out in front of him and looked down at it, tilting it, looking back at the little hatch, then at me, screwing down his eyebrows. "What the…? What do you mean!"

"That there is no reason for this hatch to open and close as it has been for the past few minutes. And look over there at that pile of rope. It is moving too. See? Looks like someone just kicked it."

"What… oh!"

"Yes. Now you see. There: the galley door is opening as well."

"Mother of God."

"Yes. Quite. Now, let's both head over and swing in that general area. Just imagine, if it were an arm moving the thing, which direction might it come from? You might have to try two directions at once!" I smiled and tapped his swords with my own.

"Yes! I see…" he headed off and swiped his swords, points down, a few inches above the floor, over the pile of rope. A black, fishy object dropped to the ground. I ran over to the window shutters and gave it a double-swipe. Montoya ran to the door and did the same. We both got the same results. Pointy tentacle stumps dropped to the deck, seemingly out of nowhere, leaking black blood at the point of severance. But this last time, it was accompanied by a response from the crew.

"Ahoy!" someone cried. The creature had doubled its efforts at the back of the ship. It was picking up crew-mates and grabbing ropes as well as kelp to entrap and strangle them. We ran to Juan Carlos, kicking in mid-air, grabbing at his throat, floating upward. We chopped all around him and he dropped. Alarcan, Casas, Handsley, and the captain, with his revolver, were all firing into the water, but to no great effect.

The rest of the crew was chopping furiously, but in their desperation, they were hacking our rigging to pieces. "Sir!" I approached Handsley in the mayhem. He looked vexed, old, sweaty. He leaned over the rails, unloading his rifle into the water. "The crew must be reminded to chop in the area of the object moving, not directly at it. We are losing valuable rigging!"

"What?" He was frustrated.

"There are tentacles controlling the kelp vines and rope flying at the crew, not only that but it – or they– are taking liberties by exploring the rest of the ship while the crew is preoccupied at the stern!"

"You – you can really see them? Don't lie or even exaggerate to me, Nickel!"

"Honestly. Not only that, but Montoya and I have just chopped the tips off a few tentacles." I grinned. "They lose their camouflage as they drop. Hideous things."

"We must tell the crew…"

"More so; we must draw the creature up from the depths and have at its brain if we are to kill it. We're doing nothing by hacking the tips. We're only annoying it. If we continue the current defenses it could last for days. Weeks. Longer. We'd all end up dead. Death by exhaustion at least."

"I agree. We need to find enough calm to regroup. I wonder what would happen if we should call a retreat. Captain!" the captain was approaching.

"Boatswain! Boatswain! This is sheer madness! They're ripping my ship to shreds! They've got no idea what they're chopping! They have no idea what they're shooting at! We've wasted the entire day chasing… phantoms! Have everyone stand down this instant!"

Handsley glanced at me. "Of course, sir. Right away!"

"Listen to me. This onslaught seems to be coming from every direction, Handsley. We need to reckon its direction. Tell them to take a break or something."

"Agreed. But sir,"

"Yes?"

"I believe the next best step would be to force the creature to the surface."

"Hm? And how might that be done."

"We could pack a charge in a barrel."

"Brilliant. A loaded barrel just might knock this thing silly. Don't we still have a carpenter?"

"Juan Carlos."

"Does he know the armory?"

"More or less. He knows gunpowder."

"Fine, fine. Have him and a few others begin right away. But we've wasted the crew as well.

We'll need to see if the monster will allow us a retreat!"

"Yes, sir! Right away! GENTLEMEN! Stop right now! Stop where you are! Put down your weapons!"

"What!" Everyone, in one manner or other, was in mid-striking pose, toppled back on one foot, hands in the air, cutting at ropes or vines, grabbing at the rigging for balance, chopping wildly into the empty air, losing their footing, leaning deep over the railing, taking aim at the moving water. Soon, they all had the message.

"LAY DOWN YOUR ARMS!"

Once they did… it was remarkably quiet. Everyone stood where they were. Kelp still flew across the ship. Ropes continued to move on their own. But without us to provoke it, the pace had slowed dramatically. Most of the confusion had been caused by the crew's desperate reaction to the events.

Handsley called us together. "We'll never kill it like this, my friends. We're only frustrating it. If there is more than one, then we'll certainly never make headway like this. Our bullets don't go that far into the water, as you well know. And gents, you're ripping our rigging to shreds each time you strike. As we mentioned before, don't swipe directly at the thing you see floating in front of you! You must aim around it," he added, with a wry smile.

"Yes!" I said uncontrollably. Handsley and the others looked at me. "Well, Montoya and I had some success by striking in two directions on either side of the object. The tip of the tentacle drops and immediately loses its camouflaging power. They're hideous."

"We noticed this too!" said Samuel. Alarcan nodded. "But we thought the black fish-like chunks had something to do with the kelp! That they somehow dropped down out of the vines."

"I wish it were so," I said.

"As do I," continued Handsley "but I'm afraid that even if we were to successfully chop at this beast we would only irritate it further by depriving it of the tips of its tentacles. We could just be trimming its fingernails for all we know."

"M-hm!" some smiled.

"The point is, and we have Nickel to thank again for making it known, that we'll need to draw it to the surface so we can do away with its brain center."

"A-hah…"

"Please give the credit to José who first suggested it," I said. They pat him on the back.

"We are going to send it a barrel loaded with gunpowder," said Handsley.

Samuel, Salvador, Alarcan, and Montoya's eyes all grew big at the sound of this. Alarcan said, "If it is an octopus, or a squid, then a well placed barrel charge could render it to mush, but if it has a brain case then we might only give it a concussion."

We turned to him, and Handsley had to ask: "What, pray tell, has both tentacles and a brain case?"

"A cuttlefish, sir. Ever eaten cuttlefish?"

"My God. It never even entered my mind," said Marques.

"It must be tremendous…" said Samuel. Long strands of kelp fell across the deck at the back of the ship. Some grappled on, some slid back into the sea. The sun was setting.

Handsley shook his head. "That's it for today, men."

"Huh?"

"That's it. Royas, Alejandro, cook us up a good meal. Go see what we have. Dredge up the rest… there's enough of it around. I want everyone in his cot tonight sleeping. We've done enough for one day. That creature isn't going anywhere and he can't get us when we're below."

"But he'll ruin the ship!" said Hernandes.

Handsley looked sternly at them. "You fellows were ripping up the ship quite well on your own. Two-thirds of today's damage was caused by the crew in your attempt to defend the ship. We can't keep that up. Besides, it would not be wise for us to tangle with this thing throughout the night. If it sleeps, let it sleep. If it stays up and ties us to the ocean floor, well then, let it. We'll just send down our loaded barrel tomorrow and cut ourselves free. Nickel, we need you to take up a watch after dinner. Ring the alarm if anything happens. The crew will be ready at first light."

"Yes sir!"

"Hoorah!" They rejoiced. Rest was well deserved.

"Drinks are on us!" yelled Alejandro and Royas, and with that, the crew followed them down to the lounge. The colors of the sunset were deepening. The ropes on deck continued to move.

XIII. THE GRANDE DAME

"Juan Carlos! Just a minute. I'd like you to take Antonio and Casas and make us up a charge in a barrel," said Handsley.

"Of course! With pleasure. If we could just sink the thing a bit… or tempt the beastie to grab at it."

"Perfect. Yes! We could bait the creature. Keep going, I like your thinking! Let this be your assignment for tomorrow morning."

"Why not tonight? We can probably have this completed within the hour."

"I want the crew to rest tonight. Including you. Go find the supplies. Use your ingenuity. Meet us in the lounge. Let me know what you come up with. Nickel! What are you doing up here?"

"Watching the monster's progress. Gauging it against a night of repose."

"Don't worry. We'll get up and fight if it tries to take us under. Just ring that alarm if we don't wake first. If it straps down the decks well then why should we chop all night if we're going to blow that monster and all its handiwork to kingdom come in the morning."

"I keep wondering... why does it want us here? What could it possibly want from us?"

"Good Lord. Who knows. Who cares. Food maybe?"

"Food... it has food. Would it be curiosity? Companionship? Control?"

"Let's discuss this over dinner. I'll be down shortly."

"Yes sir."

A single vine of kelp shot up from the water, slapped amidship, and tugged back slightly to secure hold. I walked over and kicked it. It slunk back into the ocean. The exploratory tentacles were gone. It had been baiting us. We would bait it in return. Could the monster be waiting for something? Why was it searching the ship? I picked up a lantern and went down to the hold, to listen at the keel and back by the rudder. How could the creature make no sound at all when he'd bound up the rudder last night? I must have missed something. I pressed my ear against the hull and listened, then again down at the keel.

Then I heard it. It sounded like the rubbing of heavy drapes being hung, or better yet, drapes when swept past by a gallant lady in her ball gown. So this is the monster, a ballroom grande dame sashaying about the ship, tying us to the floor of her garden. Or was it a male, perhaps? Maybe he finds the ship a curiosity and, what if he's got a collection? In the same way they find shiny trinkets in a monkey nest? Hamdoullah, we might be the newest addition to the beast's collection! Either way, it wouldn't be good. I made my way up to the lounge.

XIV. BAIT AND HOOK

"The captain has ordered a stand down! We're going to blow that thing up in the morning! What's to worry!" Samuel was yelling drunkenly at Casas. Royas had made his special grog.

"I can hear that thing swishing around outside the hold. It's unnerving," I said. I grabbed a cup and a bowl. It was fish stew.

"Well if it gets bad, just roust us and we'll come running!" said Samuel, raising his cup and looking about the room for confirmation. He was getting sloppy. At this rate, the crew wouldn't rise out of a slumber if the devil himself were to hammer on their skulls.

"Handsley, sire," said Hernandes, allowing his decorum to slip, "what is the plan and are we not going to drown in our sleep tonight? Are you, in some way, complicit with that…" he twirled his index finger, "…problem–?" He pointed to the floor. Handsley came downstairs and sat with us. Salvo snickered.

"Quiet. The captain is tired, his ship is in tatters, I'm frustrated and you are…" Handsley watched Hernandes' eyes cross, focused on the rim of his cup. "Exhausted. However, there's a good chance for wind tomorrow. That's why we'll need all hands on deck for what he has planned. We are going to rest and then we are going to wake, and be atopside, every one of us," he said pointing around the room, "at first light." A few groans emanated. "Juan Carlos and his team will ready the explosives. We'll set them alight and drop them– to stun or kill the creature, or creatures, then send down the skiff to chop us free, assuming it has done its bit to tie us to the sea floor, as it has been doing all day. Then we drop the sails, and we're off."

"Hoorah!" most yelled.

"Just like that?" said Samuel.

"Rise, boom, chop, drop, and we're off. Just like that. And we'll be armed to the teeth." said Handsley, glaring at Samuel.

"Sir." said Juan Carlos, shaking his head, "we'll only have enough powder for three barrels, at most."

"Fine. So we make 'em count. The plan is the same."

"We will need to bait the creature..." continued Juan Carlos.

"Ah. So. Tell us what you've come up with." Handsley folded his hands in front of his lips.

"Well. We were not sure what its nose or palate would prefer..."

"They have no nose" grumbled Alarcan.

"Meatballs." interjected Salvo. The group laughed.

"Er. Well. Following the idea that this being is quite possibly the largest, and master of its domain,"

"Right..."

"We imagine it has probably tasted everything in this area."

"Quite possible."

"And so, if we were to douse the barrel with chum, we'd only be adding more fish flavor to an already fishy environment."

I listened and ate my dinner quietly, wondering about the doomed creature outside.

"And so..." Handsley urged him.

"And so– what do we have, here on board, that might arouse the curiosity of a giant beastie that already has all it needs?"

"Do you know or are you asking?" Handsley was losing patience.

"Well, we thought if we could rub it with wine..."

"NO." a few voiced.

"We need that wine!" said Marques. Some laughed with him. "I'm serious!"

"Oh no no no, that would surely drive it away," said Alarcan.

"Let me finish, then, because we prefer the idea of scenting the barrel with ham. We thought a tentacled creature might like the taste." He looked around smiling. He, Antonio and Casas were pleased with themselves.

"Interesting." said Handsley. "But we'll need what little ham we have left."

"Just a corner, sir!" said Alejandro.

"That's what we didn't like about the plan," said Casas, looking at Juan Carlos.

"Indeed." said Handsley.

"Well we've been eating mostly like octopuses lately so what have we got to offer the bastard that he hasn't already tasted!" said Montoya.

Royas and Alejandro chimed in.

"Some eggs?"

"Nah." said Handsley.

"Cheese? A chunk or two, real stinky."

"Hm. Not enough. We'll need it anyway."

"Onion."

"Hm."

"Garlic."

"Hm. Keep going."

"Savory spice."

"No."

"Bay."

"No."

"Tea?"

"No…"

"Well we're not sharing this!" said Hernandes. He held his mug high and filled it off the carafe. Others did the same.

"I've got it." I said.

"What," said Handsley.

"Fatback."

"Oh?"

"Hey I'm cooking our fish in that!" said Royas.

"We won't need all of it. We'll use the old grease pot by the stove. It has a good odor and we can apply it easily to the barrels like a paste."

"Oh good!" said Juan Carlos.

"Does anyone have any objections to the fatback?" said Handsley.

"No…" said Royas and Alejandro.

"Good."

"But if we could really draw that thing up and make sure it's dead once we hit it. We must be certain." I said.

"What do you have in mind, Nickel?" said Handsley.

"Well in the skiff today, I thought that, if we could fasten our swords to the end of a few oars, we might have better reach."

"Harpoons."

"Yes. Well, spears. Would there be a harpoon on board?"

"No. But we do have a few poles in the hold. Juan Carlos?"

"Yes! If we could only jettison them into the water, I'm sure we could hang a few pulleys off the yards and bring that thing in real close."

"And cleave its filthy brain!" said Hernandes.

"Better just hook 'em to the rails. I'd hate to have that thing tearing off the yardarms. Can you have a few harpoons ready by morning?"

"In short order."

"Fine. Fine. I want everyone well rested. Whoever is finished eating, get on to your bunks immediately. We need you fresh by daybreak. Get on, now!" Some of the crew cleared the lounge.

"One more thing sir," said Juan Carlos.

"Of course." said Handsley.

"We used to make a simple harpoon launcher when I was young, with my friends, for amusement. We'd fire them at pumpkins. It was great fun." I finished my dinner leisurely. "Nickel, do we have a pencil or something? And paper?" said Juan Carlos.

"Yes. Just a minute," I pulled an old pencil stub and sheet of paper out of one of the drawers in the lounge.

Juan Carlos took them and drew a large upside down cross. "The spear fits in here, in a gully." He pointed back and forth on the long stem of the cross. "A rope, tied here and here," he pointed to the arms, "fits into a notch at the end of the spear. Rather, the spear is seated on this rope by means of a notch. Oh bother. The whole thing is tensioned and these short pieces of wood are flexible, see, and the tension is locked into place with a single peg. When the peg is removed… boom!" he sat back and smiled, pushing the paper at Handsley. "Goodness it's been a while since I've thought of that contraption! What do you think, sir?"

"I believe it's worth a try, of course!"

"It might be handy," I suggested, "with those things mounted on the rails, to have up and down movement as well as side to side, like a real whaler."

"Yes. A hinged peg." said Juan Carlos.

"Or a pegged hinge…" I said with a smile.

"Why must you always think things twice, Nickel," said Handsley.

"Well." I resented the question. I smiled. "Nervous habit."

"I can make a peg on a block. We might already have a few. All you do is peg two that match, wax 'em, then you have a hinged peg. We'll make a hole in the base of the spear thrower, and a few holes along the railing, so a team of two can move it to a new location as needed." said Juan Carlos.

"Brilliant!" said Handsley.

"It might even be fun," said Juan Carlos.

XV. THE FLASK

Juan Carlos set to work in his carpenter shack. We found ten poles down in the hold. I was, of course, drafted to his set-up crew. We delicately scooted kelp vines off the deck as they arrived. We drilled a few holes in the railing. Juan Carlos constructed the harpoon launchers entirely on his own. We fastened swords to the tips of the poles. We lashed a pulley next to each hole on the rail. The work was completed in a few hours. We stored everything in his carpenter shack, at the ready, for swift deployment in the morning.

They went to bed and I began my watch. Juan Carlos put his hand on my shoulder before heading down. "Nickel. If you need anything, anything at all, you can come get me. I'll be up right away."

"Thank you. I'll be fine. First light is…"

"…in about six hours. Yes. Take my advice and leave the kelp from now on. The monster has slowed down enough. We won't have much to chop in the morning. But in the meanwhile, don't hesitate to ring the alarm, my friend."

"Of course not."

"I hope he doesn't try any ghoulish tricks while we're away."

"Wouldn't bother me."

"Do you have enough tobacco, son?"

I felt my pockets. "Well. Now, that would bother me."

"Here." He gave me a pouch.

"Thanks."

"A nip?" he handed me his flask. I took it. He pat my shoulder.

"Cheers. I will be fine."

"Right. Good night then, Nickel."

"Good night, Juan Carlos." I took a sip of his flask. It was intensely strong, spiced rum. I could see why he'd left it with me. It had a reviving effect. Taken in small doses, I could maintain a constant, relaxed and stimulated demeanor through my watch, even though I had been up the entire day with the rest of them. I don't need that much sleep anyway.

I walked the circumference of the ship, checking the various holes in the railing, watching the starlight scatter across the water. The new moon rose. It made a puddle of light far off in the distance. At once I had an impression of the immensity of the ocean surface. I shuddered and took another sip. The water swirled nearby, so I focused my attention closer in. I changed stations. I began to think of an old chantey my uncle used to sing while gardening:

I sips me rum
'til me toes are numb
me lady's a floozie
with legs long and loozie!

Well, me friends all come
when I tips a thumb
an' we drinks our boozie
but I pats 'er bum!

Of course he was a traditional Muslim, but he'd learned the ditty in his years as a sailor and it always made him smile. He liked to tell me stories of the old days.

My reminiscing was halted by the sound of kelp slapping the deck. I was at the stern and it sounded from the bow, so I lit my pipe and made my way over. It wasn't kelp. It was three giant, fat tentacles embracing the bow. My stomach sank.

Something smacked me hard on the back of the head. A wave of hatred and frustration overwhelmed me as I struggled to maintain my footing. Purple stars rose up and surrounded me, filling the air, floating into the sky. I sank through the boards, still standing, my fists drawn. I became one with the ship, my body strong, solid and hollow. My nose stretched out far, my back was the deck, square at the keel. I felt my crew roam about me. I was scudding along with fluffy blue drifts of ocean splitting past my face, my sails fat with wind, when suddenly, all went still. I crouched, deafened, ears ringing. The water was an extension of my hearing; the water –was– my ears, akin to living in a bell jar, without walls, with no distinction between inner and outer space.

Kelp vines, thick and amber, were a forest around me, straight up from the deep, I couldn't see the bottom. It was only variations on black. An inverse sky loomed in the darkness beneath me, both suffocating and expansive. A sort of dawn erupted. Black became blue, and then I was the inverse, floating upside-down in an empty sky. The limits of my body merged with the air. I reached out into space to steady myself. My mind was flowing with information. My vision was panoramic. My arm was… a tentacle! Many tentacles; they followed my whim. My scalp pulsed, allowing water to course down upon my lungs. My fear of open spaces was gone! I felt myself enjoying expansiveness. My lungs surged. I coughed black ink. I spread my body as far as it would go. Ink filled the air. Blue faded to brown and brown faded to deep emerald green. Flies swarmed my face. Fishes pulled at my legs. Horned creatures poked at my ribs.

"Nickel! Nickel! Will someone help over here! Please!"

I opened my eyes as wide as possible but there was no day. Only dim sunlight seeped through a suffocating mass of green that deadened the atmosphere.

"Nickel! Can you hear me!"

"Yes. I hear you. Who are you."

"Will someone please help me get him down?"

I heard people talking. "There's another one over here."

"It's Casas."

"The beast hung him."

"By the blood of God."

"Hello … ?" I said. As my eyes regained focus, I found myself with limbs outstretched, suspended in the wall of a tent comprised of seaweed that had draped our ship entirely, from the masts downward. Samuel found me and tried to pull me down by the legs, but I was fastened too securely. A yardarm jabbed me in the chest as I swung there. Another voice on the ship chirped up.

"Yes I sent him up to check on Nickel. We heard a noise. I figured there was no problem! Because he didn't come get me!"

"Help."

"Hang on, man. I'll get someone."

The light on the ship was ethereal. The air inside the canopy was hot from the sun, smelly, stifling; cramped. The flies were sticking and leaving, bumbling everywhere. The crew was in a daze as far as I could tell. I saw activity but they seemed at a loss to get things accomplished.

"Gentlemen!" said the captain. "Do not trust your surroundings! Pick your way very carefully on the deck, and above all, do not disturb the canopy!"

Samuel brought José and Hernandes to cut me down. "Has he gone daft?" muttered Samuel.

"Let me check you out," said Hernandes, flipping my face back and forth by the chin. "Open your mouth."

"Jaw hurts. Chest hurts."

"Open. Close. Seems fine. You'll have a lump though, there…"

"Ow!"

"…on the back of your head. You been trying to chew your way out of here? You've got seaweed in your mouth."

"Casas was just found choked to death on seaweed, or strangled by it, or both." said José.

"My God." said Samuel, and he lifted his head back, holding on to his hat, examining the fantastic canopy that engulfed us. "We're never getting out of this."

They helped me to my feet. I found Juan Carlos' flask in my pocket, still quite full. "Liquid courage?" I rinsed and swallowed.

"Obliged." they each took a pull. Handsley approached.

"I'm having them deploy the artillery from last night. The captain says to be cautious of the canopy. The creatures are probably monitoring the outside."

"Monitoring?" said Samuel.

"Well it seems that, since they evidently would like us to stay here, it doesn't stand to reason that they would allow us to disturb their handiwork."

"Oh. Well, we're going to disturb their handiwork anyway, shortly, right?" said Hernandes.

"Patience. Wait until we have everything prepared. Royas and Alejandro brought up some corn mush and coffee. And hold off on the …

inspiration." he said, gesturing to the flask in my hand.

"It's been one hell of a night." I said.

"I understand, but we have explosives to tend to. Get some mush in you. José, Hernandes, I need you to begin work over here," he pointed. "We're hauling the barrels out next to these ramps and one over by the gate. Okay get moving. Nickel! Go eat! Marques! Yes! The long end will be aimed at the water! No, do not poke it through yet! Captain's orders!"

XVI. THE GREEN CANOPY

Handsley hissed at us. "Hold back. Just pull back. Hold it. No. Just crack it open. Make a small hole. Antonio! Watch it. Marques hang on. Let me have a look at it. Seems fine. It's bright out!" he smiled. "Okay, Marques and Antonio you are station one. You will fire only when I tell you. You will have three swords at your station, three harpoons, and two rifles. Nickel and … Alarcan! I need you to go 'round the ship and make tiny spy holes, smaller than this, and look for the monster. Take this 'scope! Report back to me."

We toured the circumference of the ship in a clockwise manner, starting at starboard of the forecastle, then bow, then port, and so on. From port, we spotted fleets of whitecaps approaching in the distance. In addition, I noticed that peering into the distance through the telescope didn't turn my stomach. The fresh air was even welcome and a relief from the cramped, fly-ridden air of our canopy.

The monster was the last thing we spotted, ironically, because it was closest to where we had started out. We found it, or them, swishing under the stern-starboard quadrant; at about seven-thirty on the clock face. We reported our findings to Handsley, whom we found by the gate at port, discussing deployment of the barrels.

"Well?"

"The water seems to be most active at the stern, starboard side."

"Good! Samuel!"

"Yes sir."

"Bring your team and set up a station at the stern, aimed starboard. Royas! Get the captain!"

"Yes sir!"

Handsley smiled. "He's been waiting to see this. Show me where you saw it. SSSHT! I need everyone to be as quiet as possible! Walk quietly! Work quietly! Captain's orders! Okay let's go."

"Sir," said Alarcan, "we also found the wind."

"You don't say. Let me see that 'scope." he walked back over to the port side and poked it through the canopy. "God-damned stinking filthy seaweed… khaa!" he spit. "I can't wait to get our ship back, men." He pressed his face right up to the canopy, holding the telescope.

"What-ho, there it is." he clapped the telescope down and put it in his pocket. "I'd say we'll have wind in an hour or so. The air smells fresh out there. We'll make it down to the westbound current in no time. All right where is that thing." We showed him the place. "Oh my God. Will you looook at thaaat!"

The monster was rippling just beneath the surface, fingering our rudder. What Handsley couldn't see were the tentacles raised in the air, gesticulating, some cruising close over our masts, others hovering at the sides. He checked through a few places in the canopy. "Where's our skiff!"

Alarcan put his eye to it. "Not far, sir, we can reel it in once we blow up the monster."

The captain stepped up to us. "I hear we're going to kill us a fish," he smiled, rubbing his palms. He pulled out his telescope. "Oh, my. Where's the barrel?"

"Here sir, we're bringing another team with a harpoon launcher, and I have men in the masts ready to cut the canopy loose…" Handsley looked down and then back at the captain. "We'll of course have the decks cleared of debris in no time. Right after the blast we'll send the skiff out to cut our hull the rest of the way free… also, Alarcan and Nickel have spotted whitecaps to the North!"

"Ah!" He rested his hands behind himself and rocked his weight from heel to toe.

"We should be free in a few hours."

"Well then! What are we waiting for?" He smiled.

"Nothing more, sir. All is in place. We were only waiting for you to arrive."

"Excellent! Let's go!"

"Hernandes. Is the barrel ready."

"Ready sir."

"José. Ignite the barrel. Montoya and Hernandes, send 'er through!"

I plugged my ears. We had put a long fuse on it. We all rushed to the canopy to watch. I saw two tentacles follow it from the ship down into the water. Then a third emerged and rolled it. The monster seemed genuinely curious. They saw the barrel submerge.

"He's taking it!" they jumped up and down. They could hardly restrain their glee.

"It's not going deep enough." said Salvador.

"Should blow soon," said Juan Carlos.

"B O O O O M ." The ship rocked. The water was alive with bubbles and wood.

"That's it!" said Hernandes, jovially.

"There it is." said Juan Carlos, smiling.

The captain spoke to Handsley: "Have someone check the hull just to be safe."

Handsley signaled the crew atop the masts. "Right away, sir!"

"Look out now!" they yelled. Chunks of the canopy began to litter the deck.

"Look out, everyone, they're chopping us free! Alejandro, check the hull for leaks below! Hurry back!"

XVII. OF INK AND WAR

All movement in the water had stopped. Only a few bubbles and some pulverized seaweed remained. We threw a line out to the skiff. The monster must have torn it loose. Handsley assigned Alarcan and me to the final chopping duties. This would be a pleasure. We brought a pole spear and a couple of swords down and pushed ourselves away from the ship. I did not need to cover my eyes nor did anyone seem to notice. Somehow, the bizarre visions of the previous night had repaired me. The open sea was no longer a threat. In fact, I was invigorated. We heard the canopy drop to the deck above.

"Ow!"

"Kick that overboard! Every last scrap! Run! Harpooners, keep your eye on the water! Where is it? Does anyone see the body?"

"No sir."

"Nickel! What can you see?"

Bubbles continued to rise from where the barrel exploded. Chunks of wood bobbed on the surface. The bubbles turned to slimy foam.

"Nothing sir, but slimy foam!"

"Quick let's get this junk chopped and get out of here!" Alarcan was uneasy. We chopped for about twenty minutes, clearing most of the hull, avoiding the blast site to the last, hoping to avoid encountering the monster's body. "There's no way it could have survived a direct hit like that, right?"

"I don't think so," I said, "Alarcan."

"Yes…?"

"What is that… what is all that?" I had the feeling we were not looking at kelp down in the water.

"Oh my God."

"What?"

"Well," he hesitated, "it looks to me like egg sacs. It was a female after all. Sea creatures sometimes attach their eggs to other living fish for safety or as a future food source. The host is often completely unaware." He shuddered. "We… are now aware."

"Handsley!" I yelled up to the ship.

"Huh?" It was Alejandro.

"Please get Handsley."

"Right away."

"I can see an ink cloud down there, too, over there." said Alarcan "Let's get this finished and get out of here."

"What!" Handsley yelled over the rail.

"It was a *She*."

He was vexed. "So what!"

"We found egg sacs attached to the back of the ship!"

"Can you cut them free?"

"We're working on it sir!"

"What's that behind you?"

I looked. The ink cloud was growing. "Ink! The body must have released some ink when it died! We think the chances are low that the beast would have survived such a direct hit!"

"Keep working. Do you need any help?"

"Don't think so, sir! Do keep a lookout over us though! It'd give us peace of mind!"

José and Salvo soon waved down at us from the rail, as they locked a launcher into place. Salvo winked at me, waving the apparatus over us. I flipped him my fist. We went back to chopping. The water around us was mostly black. Worse yet, a black mist arose from the water.

"It's wound deep around the rudder!"

"Oh God." muttered Alarcan.

"Never mind. I'll go." I jumped in and climbed down the keel. I quickly cut across a series of winds and tore us loose before the water was too black to see through. I must have been down longer than I thought. When I surfaced, I saw that the day had been completely darkened by the black mist. The captain and Handsley were standing over José and Salvo.

"Get up! Come up! Now!" yelled Handsley "We're free enough! Get that boat over to the side and lash it! Get going!"

Alarcan was nervous as well.

"What's going on?"

"Can't you hear it? That buzzing! It's back!"

"What? I was just below for a second"

"The fog has covered the ship! Look up, Nickel!"

The sun was amber. The fog was black as soot. The water had turned completely black.

"This is not good Nickel. We have to get out of this boat, now!"

"Well, help me out a little here!" We hooked her, reeled her up, lashed her in place, and all the while, the waters around us had started bubbling.

"ZZZMMMVNVVVGGZHHH."

"Oh God. It's worse!" said Alarcan.

The water was thick with ink. It dripped off the skiff in sticky lines like giant gobs of black spittle. The sooty fog had blotted out the sun entirely.

"Ready your battle stations!" yelled Handsley.

A dense cloud of flies overwhelmed the ship and over twenty rotting heads emerged from the sea. The buzzing increased intensity. The heads bobbled, perched on tentacles. Their jaws chattered incessantly. Voices sputtered from the water, indecipherable, mixing in with the buzz.

"MMMZZZVNVVZHHGHHVVV."

"GYEAAAAAGH!"

"Look! They've taken Antonio!" yelled Marques.

"Maintain your positions!" Our hearts sank but we maintained, looking every which way, as the death heads peered down upon us, flapping their jaws, pouring flies from their eye sockets. They lunged at us and pulled back like vipers. "Do not approach the rails! Back away from the rails everyone!" The air pressure suddenly changed. Our ears began ringing. We were deafened. We struggled to communicate. I was soon covered in welts. They were thick and painful, oozing dark blood. It was difficult to breathe and hard to move. I looked around me. We were, every one of us, covered in oozing welts, our body's reaction to something in the atmosphere, perhaps.

"VNVVVZHZZHHH... T U L I O ."

"Oh for God's sake they're calling the captain!" said Alarcan.

"Just ready yourself! For anything! Stay close! Take two swords! Look there! Montoya has tied swords to his arms again!"

"He is ready for war."

"As are we!"

XVIII. MUTINY AND TERROR

"VVVVZHGGHH... T U L I O ... ZZZZZJHHHVVV."

"What is happening! Alarcan stay close! Stay close!"

The captain walked toward Alejandro and Marques, aiming their harpoon at the water. He knocked them both to the deck and began beating them. He had lost his mind. By the infinite wisdom of Muhammad, we would have to mutinize the ship before the ordeal could be over. Thankfully, Handsley noticed right away. He motioned for us to keep our stations. He grabbed the captain by the shoulders to pull him off, but it wouldn't be so easy. The captain turned and swung at him, forcing blood to spill down Handsley's face. He took no notice of the injury, but used the overture as just grounds to fully launch himself at the captain, which would be a challenge anyway, in that he was a taller man, with a history of pugilism to his favor.

The captain backed up and parried. What could we do but let them go. They grappled. They tore at one another. The captain would not relent. Handsley's swollen, bloody brow limited his vision. He grabbed at the railings for support. The captain took advantage. He kicked out Handsley's legs, followed him down to the deck, and continued thrashing. Handsley, losing consciousness, managed to reach and find a stray board. He smacked it at the captain's temple, knocking him senseless. At that point, he had José and Samuel bring the captain downstairs, tie him to a pole and let him cool his heels. Handsley brought out a kerchief and went right on with his direction.

"Remember! Wait till we see some meat! Do not go near the sides yet! Watch where you walk! Look out for moving…"

"GYAAH" Samuel, on his way back up, was hit across the face with a hanging hook. He fell down cold at the door to the stairwell. His body lurched. We moved to slice him free before he was lifted out of reach.

"You stinking pile of…!" Juan Carlos ran at the railing with two swords drawn, slashing wildly in front of him. He never saw the tentacle at his ankle. It picked him up forty feet above the deck and flung him out to sea.

I sat there stupidly helping Samuel. I should have left him once he was free. I was the only one who could see it, to give them forewarning. I approached Handsley.

"Sir!"

"Nickel! Can you help?"

"Yes sir. Exactly! Place another charge where Juan Carlos was headed. You will hit the monster dead on. Then set the last one right after! If it does not kill the creature then it will certainly buy us enough time to escape!"

"Bring the barrels!"

"Where the devil is our wind!" yelled Alarcan.

"B O O M."

"The next?" Handsley looked at me. I nodded. "NEXT!"

"B O O M." The ship shivered and swayed. Tackle slapped and clanked against the masts.

Just then, the creature arose from the depths, staring fiercely down at us. This time, everyone saw it. Its camouflage had been debilitated. It appeared to the crew as a blue behemoth, with black stripes rippling down its exterior. A magnificent specimen, the likes of which no one could imagine witnessing, not even in their most cold-blooded nightmares. It had two eyes, set far apart, on either side of its head. They mounded off its face like those of a toad. It had multiple tentacles descending where its mouth ought to have been. It grabbed the ship and squeezed until we heard her hull shriek.

Montoya ran and dove off the side, at the area between the monster's eyes, swords flashing. He landed on its head and buried his swords in the creature. All three harpoon launchers fired and sank their spears deep into their mark. We had the creature tethered. Montoya worked and worked at splitting the thing's head open. We were afraid to pull it any closer to the ship. A tentacle arose and picked Montoya off like a gnat. It waved him high above the deck and swooped him down at us, to taunt us. He bravely fought to chop his way free. The tentacle wrapped his body like a boa constrictor, confining his arms. It brought him down to us, almost within reach. His face looked bloated and red. He wasn't doing well, but still, he tried to fight. We ran at the thing with our makeshift spears and fired our guns.

Another tentacle arrived from behind Montoya. It flowed into his mouth and out one of his eyes, opening his head. Then it curled and pinched his head fully off at the neck. A third tentacle poured into his chest, dismantling his body from inside, spraying our crew with gore.

His scraps were dispensed with over our heads and scattered over the water.

Suddenly, I knew what I must do. I picked up a spear, wrapped rope around it, and soaked it with the entire contents of Juan Carlos' flask. I set it alight. I ran and jumped off the rails, onto the head of the beast. The blue demon glared at me fiercely, with its pupil shaped like a fat "W," dressed in thin outlines of blue and bright orange. The wretched eyeball seemed to be fired up by lightning from within. I have never again seen such colors together or separately. I heaved my burning spear deep into the monster's pupil. There was little resistance. It burned brightly as it sank. I clung on as best I could, while it pulled my legs away with its tentacles. I grabbed the rim of its eye and held on tight. I noticed our crews' spears landing on the surface of the creature's body from up close. Chunks of flesh erupted in pits as bullet fire hailed from the ship. I shoved the flaming pole ever deeper into the eye, rocking it widely back and forth, using every last scrap of my painful body's strength. The creature flung me. I remember being airborne, upside-down, in a clear sky. The instant lasted forever.

XIX. JUST LIKE GOD

"Nickel!"

"Am I…"

"You're alive!"

"Are we…"

"We are safe! Headed south."

"Who…"

"It's me, Alarcan. We have a few left. We are all managing the ship. The captain is doing well. He's manning the helm!" he said, smiling.

"Odd. The captain…"

"Never mind. He's all right now. How's the swelling? Most of us are rid of the pain, but the sores are still there. Yours are quite bad."

"I'm okay."

"Well, you're lucky we fished you out. After it threw you, we pumped kerosene on the monster and set it on fire! The thing sank like a lead ingot. You should have seen!"

"Nice."

"Nickel, I have some bad news."

"Please, no…"

"Well, yes. You see, we had a bit of trouble with the body of Casas."

"Casas."

"Yes. He will be missed. And the others, of course. But as I said; a bit of trouble."

"Say it."

"Well we noticed his belly was distended."

"It's a corpse…"

"Unusually so. So Handsley had us open his belly. It was full of eggs. You remember we found evidence of strangulation by kelp."

"Yes. And me?"

"Yes and it looked like you'd been chewing seaweed when we pulled you down from the canopy!"

"Oh no."

"Well you were unconscious, so we couldn't really check."

"So am I–"

"You're fine now. We put a stick down your throat and you threw up about a thousand black eggs. You're the proud father of an army of monsters!"

"No…"

"Yes. And then we set them afloat in a box and burned them. So, you'll not be able to commandeer any ships with your army."

"S'too bad. I'm starving."

"Good. Hernandes said you'd probably digest the remaining few. You should be fine now. Maybe a strong shot of liquor to poison the little beasties!"

He handed me a flask. I took a sip.

"You're kidding me, right? Oh... I'm parched."

He handed me a bag of water. "No. And I will tell you briefly about the captain. He has been talking with us... since his *incident*. He described a series of dreams while we were stuck on the weed. He said a pale woman had visited him in his cabin. She told him many stories and kept him company. It was she who instructed him to attack Alejandro and Marques. We think the monster somehow had a hold of his mind."

"How... utterly... bizarre."

"Yes! And then, the wind! My God, it was, it was like God had finally come to rescue us!"

"Just like God."

"Yes!"

"Like Allah, or...?"

"Will you never rest with the jokes! Save your breath, Nickel. I'll get you some soup!"

"Fish...?"

"It's all we've got, my man."

"Oh..."

XX. EPILOGUE

I confirmed Alarcan's story of the black eggs and the captain's story of the ghost woman with other crew-mates. It was all true, unrealistic as it sounds.

As fortune would have it, regardless of whose God you pray to, we happened to run across our mizzen nest, blown off by the wind, weeks earlier, still tarped and tightly bound by yours truly. We launched a harpoon and tethered it to the aft deck to trail behind us.

While we glided along smartly, we managed to repair the rigging and included a few modifications to enable us to manage the ship with a skeleton crew. This allowed us even some daylight hours to knock about decks recreating, or to snooze our time away. Salvo shimmied down the line to the mizzen nest and splayed himself out like a starfish upon it. It was such a novel idea that we each took turns. The games advanced as we scudded along; we took to standing upon the nest and steering at the ship's wake on either side, by means of an oar, using the wake as a ramp that sent the tiny craft airborne and then landing again with a splash.

Our voyage went on like that for a week and a half until we found ourselves at a beautiful jungle island with a gentle, scooped out lagoon for us to drop anchor in. We found the jungle populated with chickens and swine. It must have been a rest stop for other weary traders, yet none so far gone as ourselves. We relaxed on coconut milk and cooked our beasts on an open fire. I ate what was given me. I thanked Allah for providence and was able to take up regular prayers once again.

Young Salvo taught us to jump from the edge of the ship and down onto the mizzen nest like a trampoline, enabling us to perform wild acrobatic feats in mid-air, landing gently in the warm, clear, bay waters. We laughed until our bellies were sore. The wretched bucket of fear and anguish, once my mortal enemy, was now no more than a makeshift circus prop.

The End

ABOUT THE AUTHOR.

Youssef Alaoui Fdili is a Moroccan American Latino. His family and heritage are an endless source of inspiration for his varied, dark, spiritual and carnal writings.

Youssef has an MFA in Poetics from New College of California, Mission District, San Francisco. There, he studied classical Arabic, Spanish baroque and Moroccan contemporary poetry. He is also well versed in 19th Century literature of the fantastic.

His writings have appeared in Exquisite Corpse, Big Bridge, (pushcart nominee at) Full of Crow, Cherry Bleeds, 580 Split, Carcinogenic Poetry, Tsunami Books and Red Fez.

youssefalaoui.info

ALSO BY THIS AUTHOR

Death at Sea - Poems
Paper Press Books & Co.

Fiercer Monsters
Nomadic Press

Critics of Mystery Marvel
2Leaf Press

Made in the USA
Middletown, DE
03 January 2023

20711879R00083